Jean Paetkau dedicates this book to Jason Sokoloski and Andrea Fajrajsl, two people who make it impossible to be bored or lonely. She wants to thank her beautiful children for sharing their giggles and inspiration in the making of this book. Also for Lola, of course.

Haley and Jacob Paetkau dedicate this book to their dad. Steve Sxwithul'txw and uncle Chris.

CONTENTS

CHAPTER 1

"Ouuuuuch!!!"

A loud cry echoed through the wooden three-bedroom house that the siblings Yacob and Baley called home. The alarming sound would have woken up anyone who was still sleeping, but since it was a school day, everyone had already said good-bye to their bed and good-morning to the kitchen table.

Yacob and his older sister Baley had obediently eaten the blueberries and oatmeal that their mother had put on the table in front of them. They no longer bothered asking why their breakfast had to be nutritious while she munched on mint chocolate chip cookies as she cut up carrots and apples for their school lunch. The last time they had attempted to explain that every human had a right to life, liberty and sugar cereals, she simply smirked and asked if they wanted to unload the dishwasher. Apparently the price for grown-up freedoms was spending the rest of your days cleaning dried spaghetti sauce from dinner plates.

"Yacob!!!!"

The second cry removed any doubt that Yacob had done something wrong. It happened a lot. Most of the time without even trying.

"You left a Slip Slider in the middle of the living room again. I stepped on it with my bare feet. I'm probably bleeding!" Yacob's sister was now hopping around on one foot while eagerly checking the bottom of her other foot for a gash.

Yacob doubted his sister was bleeding. And if she was, he would be a little bit jealous. Yacob was always looking for an excuse to use a bandage - especially in places where everyone could see them, like chins.

But Yacob knew better than to try to explain why he left his toys littered across the living room floor. That having people step on his toys and yell out in pain was exactly his plan. Especially if that person was a robber.

Yacob had tried to share his fears with his mother about thieves breaking into the house and stealing his Slip Sliders. But she usually just responded by rolling her eyes and saying she had real things to worry about, like how to tell one of her writers that their novel with 21 chapters was 21 chapters too long.

"Get into the bathroom and brush your teeth right now!" The order rang out from the kitchen where Yacob's mother was rinsing and refilling water bottles for school.

Picking up his Slip Slider from the floor and checking for damage, Yacob knew it was almost time to leave for school. Not just because he was supposed to be brushing his teeth but also because of his mother's voice. As the morning progressed, from waking up to getting on his black running shoes, his mother spoke words a little faster and a little more like the squawk of a large tropical bird. But Yacob decided that his mother was less like a bird with wings and more like a plastic wind-up toy with a spring inside that just got tighter and tighter. Yacob was worried that one day his mother's spring would be released and she would just go round and round in circles in the middle of the living room. This action would have been hilarious for a yellow bunny with giant chattering teeth, but not so much for the mom who is supposed to be in charge of everything including bedtime stories and making sure he had matching socks.

Sometimes Yacob thought his mother needed a vacation, and maybe even a healthy breakfast.

Despite the fact that his sister was already in the bathroom brushing her hair, Yacob walked in and picked up his toothbrush. Normally he would wait until she had left the room, as these days she talked a lot about "respecting her privacy," like privacy was a giant pile of leftover Halloween candy that she needed to keep hidden behind her slammed-shut bedroom door. But Yacob also knew that waiting for his nearly-teenage sister to finish brushing her hair was almost as frustrating as waiting for a new Slip Slider to arrive in the mail. He was also worried that if he didn't brush his teeth right away his mother's voice would go from parakeet to cockatoo.

Yacob brushed his teeth as quickly as possible but not so quickly as to end up being sent back to the bathroom to brush them again and "properly this time!"

Putting his toothbrush back into a cup on the counter, Yacob stood on the tips of his toes and bent over the sink so he could drink directly from the tap. With his mouth positioned under the end of the silver faucet, he turned the tap with his right hand and waited for the water to rush out.

At first there was only a gentle noise of the pipes gurgling, like how his stomach sounded after eating too much ice cream before bedtime. But then suddenly, a few inches in front of Yacob's startled eyes, a rapid cascade of bubbles poured out of the faucet. Only lightning reflexes prevented the almost eight-and-a-half year old from ending up with a mouth full of bubbles. But even with his lips firmly pressed together, Yacob inhaled in surprise, and one small bubble got sucked up his nose. Stepping back in shock, Yacob released a blasting sneeze in the room that was rapidly filling with glistening soapy spheres.

"What the heck?" Baley yelled out in reaction to the explosive sound of Yacob's sneeze.

Turning away from the long wall mirror into which she had been gazing intently while brushing her chestnut hair, Baley was struck speechless at the site of bubbles bouncing dozily off the bathroom walls and floors.

The bubbles made no apologies for their sudden appearance and simply floated around the room with a lazy kind of confidence. Yacob and Baley looked at each other in disbelief while bubbles bounced off their heads without popping.

And then abruptly, before either of the siblings had a chance to share the questions that were filling up their brains as quickly as the room was flooding with bubbles, the door flung open and all the bubbles exploded at the exact same moment. Like all the little bubble brains were acting in unison.

Standing at the door with one hand still on the silver knob, Yacob and Baley's mother opened her mouth as if to speak. But something about the stunned looks on her children's faces made her think twice about launching into another speech about hair and socks and backpacks being packed. Instead, her eyebrows knit together as she looked carefully first at Yacob and then at Baley, who was still holding up her hairbrush like a purple weapon she was using for protection.

Finally, their mom just shook her head and quietly mumbled, "Get in the car." Then she spun around and walked away.

Knowing that their mom was waiting, and that her patience was running out like a mostly empty jar of jam that clangs when you put the knife back in, Yacob and Baley turned to each other with wide eyes.

"What ....?" started Baley.

"....was that?" finished Yacob

"Bubbles!?" Baley stated.

"Everywhere!" Yacob confirmed.

Yacob's sister then asked, "What did you...?"

"What? What did I do? I was brushing my teeth!" Yacob exclaimed while pointing at his toothbrush as if offering proof. Even though he was used to getting blamed for everything that went wrong, Yacob was almost sure the bubble extravaganza was not his fault.

Finally Baley put down her hairbrush and pointed an accusing finger at Yacob. "We will talk about this later."

Left alone in the bathroom after his sister had marched out, Yacob turned around in a circle while looking up and down, as if the walls and floors might offer some clues to the bubble mystery.

Making his way to the front door, he remained in a daze while tying his shoes and shrugging on his backpack.

Once he was out of the house and was walking along the gravel driveway to the car, Yacob's mind replayed images of bubbles bouncing off the sink, the toilet seat and his sister's nose. Lost in his own thoughts and confusion, he at first ignored the snicker and titter of hushed giggles coming from behind the overgrown bushes in his front yard. Turning his head in the direction of the sound, he spotted the flash of a floppy red triangle disappearing around the corner of his house.

Although he was almost eight-and-a-half years old, Yacob had a sudden longing for the security blanket he had given up before starting kindergarten. But on this day of extra peculiar and very unexplainable events, Yacob instead reached for the familiar touch of the Slip Slider in his coat pocket. And as his mother drove along the still quiet streets to school, Yacob rubbed the cool metal until it turned warm and comforting to the touch.

CHAPTER 2

With Yacob's bum firmly planted in his blue plastic chair, his Grade 3 teacher, Mr. Beverage, stood at the front of the classroom and explained multiplication by the number four in his chirpy, singsong voice. Mr. Beverage might actually have been extra pleased with his student's focus on school work that particular morning in early November. For once, the almost eight-and-a-half year old wasn't constantly wiggling and his eyes were fixed front. However, the reason Yacob's arms and legs were so still was because his mind was so busy. His body may have been in school, but his brain refused to join him.

Visions of bubbles, small and enormous, floated in front of his eyes. But now the extra peculiar and unexplainable events of the morning were stirring up his imagination. Instead of just seeing empty bubbles drifting around his bathroom at home, he was picturing giant glistening spheres capturing and carrying away some of his favourite toys. A hamster stuffie that he sometimes still kept under his pillow at night was caught in one of the looming bubbles, a breeze pushing it just out of Yacob's reach.

"What do you think about bubbles?" Yacob had escaped from the classroom for first recess and was trying to talk to his best friend about what happened that morning without telling her what had happened that morning.

"Bubbles?" Hayda shrugged. "They're OK, I guess. Kind of Grade 2-ish, though. If you know what I mean."

"Totally," nodded Yacob in eager agreement, not wanting his friend to think he was planning to rent a bubble blower for his next birthday party. Feeling that his coolness might now be in doubt, Yacob thought it was time to add a hint of danger.

"But do you think they might be evil?" he asked, then took another bite of his apple and cinnamon granola bar.

"Evil?" Hayda said with interest, as though this might be the best thing that ever happened to bubbles. Evil was definitely an upgrade. "Wow. Never imagined that." And then after another thoughtful pause she continued, "What kind of evil? Like, what would they do?"

Yacob continued to chew, giving himself time to come up with an answer.

Remembering the images that were passing through his mind while his teacher was explaining the multiplication magic of the number four, Yacob first offered, "Stealing your favourite stuffies?"

The doubtful look on Hayda's face made it clear she wasn't overly impressed by the terror of the toy-napping bubbles, so he added, "And then taking them through a portal which no human can cross."

Hayda's eyes widened with excitement, letting Yacob know his story had struck home.

Picking up the thread of Yacob's imagination, Hayda continued, "And what if the bubbles also capture real animals like cats and racoons and a baby deer. What about if the evil bubbles even took Spelunky!"

Spelunky was Hayda's Sheepadoodle, a mixed breed dog that liked to chase tennis balls and lick the faces of children when they were crying.

Hayda was really warming up to the exploits of the evil bubbles and she took in a deep breath before exclaiming, "What about parents? They might steal our parents!"

"But humans can't pass through the portal," Yacob quickly reminded her. After all, rules were rules, even imaginary ones.

"Are parents human?" Hayda wondered out loud, "Sometimes I'm not sure."

Yacob decided it was time to take back control of the bubble adventure. In the first place, he was the one who had actually seen bubbles in his bathroom this morning. Secondly, everyone knows the other side of portals are deep and dark spaces with lots of blinking stars but absolutely no chocolate chip mint cookies. Not the kind of place you want to send your mother. Even if she made you eat Brussels sprouts on Thanksgiving.

However, just as Yacob was trying to steer the ship that was Hayda's imagination into slightly calmer waters, he spotted a shark on the horizon. Well, less of a shark and more like his sister. And obviously a real sister was much scarier than a pretend shark. Especially when she was swimming straight for Yacob.

Baley loomed over her brother, who was sitting on the grass in the field.

"You have my water bottle," she stated in a matter of fact tone.

His sister offered no explanation and none was needed. Their mother was famous for packing her children's favourite fruit or cookies in the wrong lunch kit. Mixing up water bottles was a weekly occurrence.

Yacob scrambled to retrieve his sister's purple water bottle from his backpack, hoping he was quick enough to prevent Hayda from saying whatever she was going to say next.

He wasn't.

"I don't think Spelunky would like to be carried away in a bubble. He went on a plane once and he hid in the closet for two days afterwards. He only came out when we made him a plate of bacon. And we could never use the closet again."

Baley looked at her brother with concern, "Bubbles? Why are you talking about bubbles?"

Yacob flashed a weak smile at his sister. It was a smile he normally saved for his mother when he had no excuse to explain certain unfortunate events. Like a bottle of glue being in the pocket of his pants that went through the laundry. Or how honey ended up on the toilet plunger.

"Hey Hayda, I saw a lizard climbing up the wall outside the kindergarten classroom. It was purple," stated Baley. Yacob was always impressed by his sister's ability to lie without blinking.

"A purple lizard? There are no purple lizards. Not on this continent. No recorded sightings anyway."

Hayda was famous at school for her love of lizards. Her backpack had a giant chameleon on the front pocket and she had little lizard erasers in her pencil case. Last Halloween she even went as an Italian wall lizard, which mostly made her look like a green zebra that had been turned into a breakfast sausage.

Without asking if Yacob was coming, Hayda took off in the direction of the made-up lizard sighting. An evil, toy-stealing bubble was no competition for a possibly undiscovered species of lizard.

Yacob braced himself for what was coming next.

"Look Yacob, don't talk about bubbles," his sister commanded.

"Not small bubbles, not big bubbles. Not bubbles in your soda. Not even bubble baths."

Yacob nodded in agreement. He knew that at this moment actually replying to his sister was unnecessary and possibly even dangerous.

"And just remember, if you start walking around talking about bubbles in our bathroom, people are going to think you are …." Baley left the sentence unfinished. Like the last word had fallen off a cliff. "Well, you know what they will think you are. And it's not good."

With those words of warning still hanging in the air, Baley turned on her heels and marched across the school yard. Her purple water bottle swung energetically in her hand like it was a baton, as if she was a leader of an invisible, slightly angry, marching band.

Yacob actually had no idea what people would think if he talked about bubbles in the bathroom. But his sister's threat was enough to keep the word bubbles off his lips for the rest of the day. But unfortunately, her warning only made it more impossible to keep images of shiny spheres from drifting through his mind.

So when Yacob walked through the front door of his home that afternoon he let out a huge sigh. The almost eight-and-a-half year old was relieved that he had managed to get through the whole day without accidentally talking about bubbles with a classmate. But as the one threat faded, another quickly took its place. And it was a much more urgent disaster. Like going from worrying about a sunburn to the fact that there was a giant, burning meteor hurtling towards your house. Or the kitchen specifically.

Yacob's mother was unpacking their lunch kits on the counter. She was about to rinse them off in the sink and put them into the dishwasher.

"No!" yelled Yacob, standing in the hallway with his coat and shoes on.

His mother and sister turned in his direction, their faces full of surprise and concern.

Then his sister's face lit up with understanding, as she realized what Yacob was yelling about.

"Mom, Yacob just remembered that there is something wrong with the taps, I mean the water, or probably the entire sink actually," Baley stumbled over the words. Her second attempt at lying in one day wasn't going that well.

"You crazy kids." Their mom shook her head as she dismissed her children's warnings. "There is nothing wrong with the sink or the water." And before they could offer another yelp or perhaps just a better lie, Yacob's mother reached over the sink and turned on the tap.

"Water! It's water!" shouted Yacob with glee.

His mother gave Yacob another puzzled look, "What were you expecting? Syrup? Gravy?"

Baley jumped in to respond for her brother, "Oh, it was nothing mom. We've just been watching a new show, 'Disasters in Your Kitchen!' Kind of like a cooking show, but instead of meals, you make explosions."

"Well, as long as it isn't too scary for Yacob. You know he gets nightmares," his mother cautioned while continuing to wash off their school containers.

Yacob wondered whether there was an Olympics for lying. Despite her earlier stumble, he thought Baley had a shot at a gold medal.

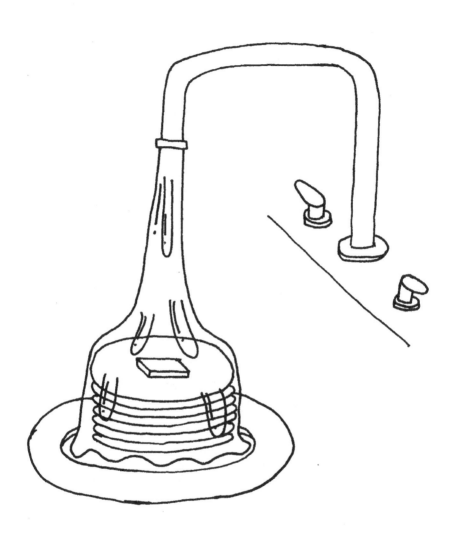

CHAPTER 3

"Can you please try to kick the ball in a way that is not so expectable?"

Baley easily caught the soccer ball under her right foot before booting it back in Yacob's direction.

It was Saturday morning and the two siblings were in their backyard playing soccer. They had made a deal. Yacob would help his sister practise goaltending before her indoor soccer tryouts next week. In exchange she had promised to battle Slip Sliders with him after lunch. But standing in wet leaves while his sister yelled at him made Yacob wonder whether the deal had actually been a good one. He was also very tired this morning. Last night he kept waking from restless dreams, as his brain continued to grapple with the extra peculiar and unexplainable events of the previous day.

After they had arrived home from school Friday afternoon and their mother had used the kitchen sink without disaster, Yacob and his sister had quietly made their way to the bathroom and locked the door behind them. Their mother was too busy complaining to the kitchen walls about the chunks of wet toast she had to clean from the bottom of the dishwasher to notice their strange behaviour. Yacob was glad for his mother's sake that the kitchen walls were such good listeners.

Standing with her back almost touching the bathroom door, Baley had nodded at Yacob and then at the sink. Yacob wasn't sure why he was the one who had to try the taps again. In most of the stories he read, older people were supposed to take care of younger ones. As he prepared to be swallowed up by a giant bubble and carried away through a portal that maybe humans could pass through after all, he guessed his sister hadn't read those books.

With one hand gripping the Slip Slider in his pocket for courage, Yacob had reached forward with the other hand and had very gently turned the tap on. He leapt back as the same tummy-gurgling noises came from under the sink and then, very slowly, three small bubbles were released out of the end of the spout. After that there was a short pause of nothing, followed by the gush of regular water pouring from the silver spout.

In silence Yacob and his sister Baley had watched the three bubbles bounce around the bathroom. The bubbles were so strong that the two children could actually hit them back and forth to each other. But then, once again, when Baley opened the door, the three bubbles burst at the same time. And for the rest of the evening, when Yacob or Baley had tried the bathroom taps, only water streamed out. Yacob was both slightly relieved and very disappointed by this turn of events.

The slap of the soccer ball against the wall of the house on that cool Saturday morning let Yacob know he had missed another kick from his sister. He turned to watch as the black and white sphere rolled along the yard's gravel edge and came to rest under the outdoor tap for the house.

"Yacob, hurry up," he sister nagged in an irritated tone that older siblings only used with their younger siblings. Even when they were doing them a favour.

Responding to his sister's command, Yacob started walking across the lawn. However, before he reached the soccer ball, another player entered the game. And this uninvited member of the opposing team started rubbing its furry face and body all over the

16

ball, as though soccer balls were made for tickling not kicking. The soccer ball didn't seem to mind this upgrade in treatment, but the siblings certainly did.

"Cat!" yelled Baley.

"Shoo!'" shouted Yacob

The orange and black tabby stopped to stare at the two children. He gave them a look that reflected annoyance more than fear, as though Yacob and Baley were interrupting his fun, not the other way around. Then, after taking a brief moment to ponder his next move, the cat pranced off with his tail and nose in the air. He was clearly in search of another yard with another ball for rubbing that didn't have such yelly children in it.

Still standing between the recycling bin and a large garden pot that were the makeshift goal posts, Baley called out to Yacob, "Wash it off!" She paused and then added a "please."

Yacob's sister had a severe allergy to cats. One touch and she would sneeze through an entire box of tissues and her body would be covered in hives. She had once visited a friend's house and sat on a pillow that was actually a cat bed. By the time his sister arrived home she looked like a human candy cane, with tiny polka dots instead of stripes.

Moving the ball so that it was directly under the garden tap, Yacob turned on the faucet without thinking. But what happened next made him leap back in surprise.

"What's wrong?" called out Baley, but Yacob didn't bother to answer. The bubbles pouring out of the spout offered all the reply that was necessary.

Baley ran over to stand next to her brother as a seemingly endless supply of bubbles filled the yard around them.

And then they heard a yell. A yell that was both big and small. Or rather a yell that belonged to someone both grown up and not grown up at all. In other words, a very tiny grandpa. In a red hat. With a red face.

"Turn off the river maker!" yelled the knee-high creature with more authority than you would expect someone the size of a coffee maker to possess. "You are going to be running down the magic!"

Yacob, who was not used to taking orders from people shorter than him, decided it was still best to obey. The little man's face was now redder than his hat, and it didn't look healthy.

Once Yacob had turned off the tap, the man clapped his hands together twice, and instantly all the bubbles in the backyard vanished.

Then Yacob, Baley and the extra peculiar and unexplainable creature in a red hat stood in a triangle and stared at each other. Yacob was relieved to see the wrinkly face slowly fade to a lighter shade of ketchup.

Baley stepped forward to get a closer look at this garden invader, making Yacob unexpectedly grateful that he wasn't an only child. He thought he was probably extra lucky that his sibling was a girl too. His friend Grandon had an older brother who once put his underwear in the freezer. When Grandon finally discovered his underwear stuffed between packs of frozen blueberries, they were icy and hard and smelled a little bit like fish.

"Are you a garden gnome?" Baley had always taken the fastest route between a question and an answer even if it wasn't the most polite.

"A garden gnome? A garden gnome?!!!!" shrieked the small being in response.

Yacob was distressed to see the colour of the creature's face once again change to match his red hat.

""Please do not be using this name. It is a most insult. I come from a long line of the ancient and the wise. We are known to be called Snufflewort!"

Before he could catch himself, Yacob let out a snort of laughter. He wasn't sure how wise these creatures were if they thought the name 'Snufflewort' was an improvement on 'garden gnome.' Snufflewort sounded like a lumpy growth on your toe that occasionally caught a cold.

"But you are the … the things that, you know, sit in gardens. Like decorations," continued Baley, unfazed by the outraged Snufflewort.

Shaking his head, the Snufflewort took off his red pointed hat, scratched his white hair, and then put his hat back on. He was much calmer when he finally responded to Baley.

"This was our way of being among Rumpa. We are liking the garden spaces. Rumpa are liking us in their garden spaces. It was an arrangement most pleasing to everyone," the Snufflewort explained.

"What's a Rumpa?" Yacob finally found the courage to put his first question to the creature.

"That's obviously us," Baley informed him, "they are the snifflethingys and we are the rumps."

Baley turned back to the Snufflewort and asked, "And then something changed? With the garden situation?" Yacob's sister had a nose for smelling trouble. The way that Yacob's ears could hear a bag of potato chips being opened two rooms away.

But before the Snufflewort could respond, their mother's voice rang out from the kitchen window.

"Yacob! Baley! Time for lunch!"

The Snufflewort looked around with fear, and then quickly continued. "You do not need to be knowing the whole of the happy then sad story of Snufflewort. You only need to be leaving the magic alone!"

"What magic?" inquired Yacob.

"The magic in the water," replied the Snufflewort.

"You mean the bubbles?" Yacob asked with growing excitement.

"Rumpa are using the name bubbles. But bubbles are games for the children. Like rubbery toys that make the burping sound when you are squeezing the belly. For us they are having the name circle wafters."

"Circle waffles, bubbles, whatever," Baley continued in a matter of fact tone. "We'll lay off the taps, but you are going to make us a deal."

Yacob almost wanted to warn the Snufflewart that making deals with his sister didn't always turn out the way you might expect. But his first loyalty was to Baley, not to a miniature grandpa with a long beard and red pointy hat.

"We want you to meet us, at dusk, at this spot. And we are going to need more information," Baley finished with a warning.

"Or else?" demanded the Snufflewort. Clearly his ancient and wise ways didn't prepare them for negotiating with Yacob's sister.

"Or else we tell our Rumpa mother," Baley stated while pointing at the kitchen window. "We tell her everything."

"Oh no, we are not allowed to have talking with the giant Rumpa! It's very written in the book of *Things Snufflewort Can and Can Not Do*. If there is danger that is growing larger, we can make the talking with small Rumpa. But never the giant ones, who are wearing shoes the size of our heads."

The Snufflewort took a gulp of air, like he was trying to swallow a growing panic.

"It is agreed. At dusk, we will be returning to this place in the grass. But you must promise to share our talking with no one. Especially no one who is a giant Rumpa."

And having made that reluctant deal with Yacob's sister, the Snufflewort touched his nose and let out a sneeze. The sneeze was so loud that both Yacob and Baley blinked with surprise.

By the time they had unblinked their eyes back open, the red hat and its owner were gone.

CHAPTER 4

The Slip Slider zoomed down the launching tunnel to land in the battle pad and crash against its challenger. The first of the two Slip Sliders to lose all three rings would be kicked out of the competition. Yacob's red and black Slider had already knocked the first ring off his sister's royal blue contender. A small smile formed on Yacob's lips. It was the smile of a younger sibling who might finally have a victory over an older one.

Despite the fact that the morning had included even more extra peculiar and unexpected events, Yacob was pleased that his sister had kept her promise to play Slip Sliders after lunch. He could be wrong, but even his fearless sister seemed to want some company after the appearance, firstly, of the bubbles, and secondly, of the Snufflewort.

"Why meet at dusk?" asked Yacob over the noise of the Sliders crashing into each other.

Baley took a breath before beginning her explanation.

"Everything amazing happens at dusk. The sun sets, the moon comes up. Halloween and Christmas Eve start at dusk, and campfires are definitely the best at dusk."

Yacob was impressed. To him dusk meant going to bed. Which was the most boring thing that happened every day of his life.

There was a small ding as one more of Baley's Slip Slider rings was knocked off and landed next to Yacob's foot. But Baley did not seem bothered by the poor performance of her Slider so far.

Grabbing her eliminated ring from the floor, she continued sharing her theory. "Basically, if you are going to start a new adventure, it should happen at dusk. If there was a contest for the coolest time of the day, dusk would win."

"But what are we going to tell mom?" Yacob asked. "About wanting to go outside that late?"

Before replying, Baley tilted her head to the side, a sign that she was carefully considering Yacob's question.

"We will tell her that we just want to play a little more soccer together before bedtime."

"Will she believe that? Sounds a little hokey," responded Yacob with doubt.

"It is hokey. But she won't question it," Baley said with confidence. "Parents always say yes to anything involving exercise and not involving TV. For the entire history of parents it has always been that way. And also, if it includes two siblings getting along, well that is literally the ultimate parent fantasy. Right after getting to sleep-in on a weekend."

"Wow, you sure know a lot about parents."

Baley nodded in agreement, "Actually, they are quite fascinating, if you can forget how totally boring they are."

And Baley was right.

After dinner, when the siblings asked if they could go outside for another hour, their mother stopped only briefly from once again loading the eternally demanding dishwasher to smile in their direction and nod in her absent-minded way, "That sounds nice.

Make sure to wear a hat please. It's cool in the evenings now."

Once they were outside, Baley and Yacob were a little uncertain as to how they should proceed. Did they need to summon the Snufflewort? Or could the ancient and wise creatures simply feel the presence of the young and curious kids?

It turns out they didn't have to wait long.

While they were both facing the outdoor tap, trying to stand in almost the same spot as when they first met the Snufflewort, they suddenly heard someone clearing their throat behind them.

When the siblings turned around there were two Snufflewort staring at them from the middle of the yard. One was the Snufflewort they had met that morning. The other had on a dress, their hair was in two braids and they also had a long white beard.

"Good evening Rumpa girl and Rumpa boy," said the Snufflewort they met before.

"Hi, again," responded Yacob's sister. "I'm actually Baley and this is Yacob. Do you have names?"

They Snufflewort they already knew replied, "The name I have is Bob. And this is Cosimo."

"Bob?" Baley had a look of disbelief on her face. "For real?"

"What are you expecting?" demanded the Snufflewort named Bob, sounding slightly offended.

Baley shrugged her shoulders, "I don't know, maybe something that sounds a little more … historic or important. I think the guy who fixes my dad's car is named Bob."

"To be keeping a Rumpa car in good running motion seems like a job of very high importance. Worthy of someone who is carrying the name Bob," responded the Snufflewort with pride.

"I once was crawling into the trunk of a Rumpa car," bragged the Snufflwort named Cosimo. "It was the most exciting time of my 300 years."

Baley sighed with a hint of the irritation she usually saved for dealing with her little brother. "Well, Bob and Cosimo, it's very nice to meet you and to hear about your love of automobiles, but it's almost bedtime for us. So what's the scoop with the bubbles or circle wafters coming out of the tap? Actually, more importantly, what's the scoop with you? Have garden gnomes, I mean Snufflewort, always been able to talk? Where do you come from? Do you like pizza?"

"These are all questions of importance. Especially about pizza. Are you making to order some? We are preferring thin crusts. Vegetarian, obviously," said Bob.

"No, I am not ordering pizza," replied Baley. "I don't have any money. Or a phone for that matter."

"Oh," responded Bob, clearly disappointed in his new acquaintance. "That's too bad. I always prefer adventuring when my tummy is full."

"Adventure?" Yacob finally found his voice in the growing darkness of the backyard. "What kind of adventure?"

Bob turned to the Snufflewort with the braids and beard and said, "I have made a decide it is the time to show the tragedy of incredible sadness."

"But they are Rumpa. How are we knowing if they have worth of our trust?" said Cosimo. "The danger is already big and great!"

"In the book of *Things Snufflewort Can and Can Not Do* it allows asking of help from small Rumpa when there is a great time of need," replied Bob.

"But what if they share the talking with a giant Rumpa?" responded Cosimo, whose arms were starting to flap with alarm.

Yacob heard his sister exhale loudly before interrupting the bickering creatures.

"Speaking of rules and giant Rumpa, have I mentioned that my mother always follows the rules about bedtime? In fact, if we aren't inside the house pretty soon, she is going to come out here with a humongous gong and a flashing light on her head calling our names."

At first, Yacob giggled at this wild version of his mother. But then he looked at his sister with puzzlement. They may have a large frying pan in the house, but there was no humongous gong. As an almost-eight-and-a-half year old, he wouldn't have overlooked a treasure like a gong. Then he remembered that his sister had a gold-star in lying. If they gave gold stars for lying, that is.

In response to Baley's words, the Snufflewort named Bob snapped to attention. He had clearly made a decision.

"Follow me," ordered Bob. "And try to become a smaller than you are."

Yacob wasn't sure how to make himself smaller so he decided staying quiet was the next best thing.

Bob led the two children and the second Snufflewort through a hole in their fence, across their neighbour's dried up strawberry patch, and into a yard that was two houses away. Yacob immediately felt uneasy. They were standing behind the home of Grumpy Schlumpy.

Since the start of forever, or at least since humans lived in houses, on any street where children live, there is always one oldish neighbour like Grumpy Schlumpy. A neighbour who yells if a ball rolls on their grass, like grass is a treasure that is better than chocolate ice cream. A person who never says hello just because the sun is shining, or tells you stories about back-in-the day. The Grumpy Schlumpies of this world only occasionally peek out from between their dusty curtains with an angry face to let you know that whatever you are doing, it is the wrong thing to be doing. And there is one absolute rule. You never go in the backyard of a Grumpy Schlumpy.

Yacob looked at his sister for a sign that everything was OK, but to his horror, his never-afraid sister actually looked a little nervous.

"You must be coming this way," whispered Bob, motioning for the group to follow him down the cement path that ran along the side of the house.

The last thing on earth Yacob wanted to do at that moment was to get even closer to the house of Grumpy Schlumpy. But as his sister and the other Snufflewort started to follow Bob, Yacob knew that the other last thing on earth he didn't want to do was to be alone in the backyard.

The quiet parade of small and tall creatures walked softly along the path until Bob held up his hand to stop. He then waved to the group to gather around a tiny, square window that was just above ground level.

Wiping away spiderwebs, Bob pointed for the two children to peak inside.

At first Yacob and Baley couldn't make out anything in the darkness. Was it a bunch of oversized roses wilting out of a lumpy vase? A collection of discarded red vacuum cleaners?

But then slowly shapes took form in the gloom of the basement. Sticking out of the top of a large burlap sack, with the word "junk" taped to the front, were the heads of five dejected looking Snuffle-wort. With their hats at a tilt which matched their sad frowns, the Snufflewort looked like they would never decorate a yard of fresh spring grass again.

In the growing shadows, Yacob watched as one Snufflewort mouthed a silent word. Yacob would bet his very best Slip Slider that the word the sad creature had spoken was 'help'.

CHAPTER 5

"How do you think they got there?" Yacob whispered into the walkie talkie he was clutching under his blanket.

His mother had long since closed the door to her bedroom, and was probably already fast asleep. Yacob wasn't usually awake when his mother was not. It gave him a slightly unsettled feeling in his belly. Like someone had turned out the light of the lighthouse. He clutched the electronic device a little tighter and waited for the reassuring sound of his sister's voice to come through it.

"I don't know. But it is the basement of Grumpy Schlumpy, so maybe they stepped on his grass," replied Baley. "You know how he is about his grass."

After peering at the sack of helpless Snufflewort slumped next to wooden chairs and stacks of old cookie tins earlier that evening, the children and their two new companions quietly skittered back to the safety of their own yard. But before the siblings could ask the questions that were racing from their brains to their lips, their mother called for them to come inside. And with a sneeze that made Yacob and Baley violently blink, the two Snufflewort once again vanished.

"Actually, I think I remember something interesting." Baley's voice came out of the walkie talkie. "I think Grumpy Schlumpy used to have garden gnomes. This was a million years ago, like when you were only 1 or 2 years old."

Yacob had never been included in a back-in-the-day story before. It made him feel important and just a little bit older. He wondered if he would be able to grow a beard soon, like his new friends.

"So what happened?" Yacob asked in an excited whisper.

Baley responded, "I don't know. Maybe the basement happened."

At that point the two siblings grew quiet, imagining all the years of their mostly carefree childhood that the Snufflewort had been trapped in a sack in the basement of Grumpy Schlumpy. Yacob used to think being shipwrecked on a desert island without his Slip Sliders and his mom was the worst thing that could happen to him. But thoughts of the shadowy basement were making him reconsider his worst-things-possible options.

Finally Yacob spoke, "I wonder how we can rescue them."

"Rescue them? Who said anything about rescuing them?" demanded Baley.

Yacob didn't understand his sister's question. This was obviously a situation that called for rescuing. A dark basement that could be a dungeon, small innocent creatures with pointy hats held captive, and a grumpy if not completely evil owner of the dark basement that could be a dungeon. It was like a recipe for a rescue. In fact, he wouldn't be surprised if a dragon showed up soon.

Yacob decided he must actually be a little bit older and wiser if he needed to explain the situation to his sister.

Pressing down the 'talk' button on his walkie talkie, Yacob said, "Why do you think the Snufflewort let us see them? They need help getting their friends out of the basement of Grumpy Schlumpy. They can't defeat the evil dungeon-keeper on their own!"

"Evil dungeon-keeper? Wow, I just thought we had a cranky old man who doesn't give out Halloween candy living on our street. But evil-dungeon keeper? I could sell tickets to that, give tours to my friends even," said Baley thoughtfully.

Even though Yacob had heard that grown-ups often only cared about money, he hadn't expected his sister's soul to be at risk before she even got her braces off.

"This isn't a chance to get rich," scolded Yacob. "It is a chance to be a hero!"

Baley sighed heavily into her walkie talkie. "I suppose so, although I am still wondering how the bubbles come into it."

That thought made Yacob grow silent. He hadn't read any stories that involved both dungeons and bubbles. That was like putting alligators and space creatures in the same cartoon. It was two different universes smashing together.

Saying goodnight, the siblings were now both lost in their own thoughts. For Yacob this involved images of dungeons and neighbours who were actually ogres. Eventually he drifted off to sleep, only to dream about dragons who blew bubbles instead of fire.

After finishing breakfast the next morning, the two siblings headed out into the garden without any need for discussion. Humankind, or at least Snufflewort-kind, was depending on them.

"Smash the basement window and lower a ladder into the room!"

The Snufflewort had shown up in their usual mysterious manner soon after the two children arrived in the backyard."

"But someone must be having the courage to enter the dark chamber to be releasing the sack's top rope from our fellow Snufflewort."

Yacob, Baley and the two Snufflewort were brainstorming ideas for rescuing the creatures who were being held captive.

"What about sending Grumpy Schlumpy a letter saying there is a special package at the post office he needs to collect," offered Yacob. "Then his house will be empty."

"What kind of the special package?" asked Bob.

Yacob thought for a moment, "Maybe a pirate treasure."

Cosimo shook his head, "I don't have thinking giant Rumpa are the same in love with treasure as much as small Rumpa. This also has truth with candy. It is one of the many sensible reasons we are having no trust for giant Rumpa."

This information was confusing for Yacob. Since grown-ups were very interested in money, why wouldn't they be eager to get their hands on treasure? He guessed it was just one of those opposite things that happens with adults. Like how his mom said that television cooked your brain into mush. But the only times she really laughed these days was when she was watching one of her comedy shows from back-in-the-day.

"But I think Yacob may be on to something," said Baley, returning Yacob's thoughts to the basement mystery that needed solving.

Using her brother's idea as a starting point, Baley began to sketch out a possible rescue plan. As they listened with intense focus, the Snufflewort started to wave their arms in excitement. The one with braids even did a little dance in a circle after Baley finished talking.

With the four creatures in agreement that they would attempt to complete the Freedom-For-Snufflewort rescue mission the next weekend, Yacob waited for the creatures to sneeze and then disappear. He was determined not to blink his eyes this time. But his sister wasn't done yet.

"One more thing," began Baley with a determined voice, "If we are going to risk going up against Grumpy Schlumpy to save your friends, I think it is only fair if we get a few more details."

The Snufflewort named Bob replied, "What kind of the details?"

"All of them," answered Baley. "Where do you come from? Why

don't you hang out in gardens much anymore? How did the Snufflewort end up in the basement of our nasty neighbour? And for that matter, why are there unusually strong bubbles you call circle wafters coming out of our taps? But only when kids turn them on, not grown-ups?"

The Snufflewort named Bob gave Baley a serious look. But instead of replying to her questions, he simply reached into his beard with his right hand. When his hand reappeared from the white tangle of hair, it was holding a long tea-coloured scroll. Yacob noticed that the rolled up paper was actually much longer than the beard itself, so he wasn't sure how it had remained hidden inside. But his mom's purse worked the same way - it could hold extra lunches and drinks, spare clothes and even emergency stuffies for visits to the dentist.

"I have expecting such questions from a Rumpa who is young but is also much wise," stated the Snufflewort. "I have done the writing down of our story for your reading."

Bob then handed the scroll to Baley, who accepted the important looking paper with two hands. And then before Yacob could remember not to blink, the Snufflewort sneezed.

CHAPTER 5 ½

The Happiness then Sad Story of the Snufflewort

Snufflewort are being the creatures born from the land of clover trees in the summer bright and winter snow blanket. In the earlier memory of their existing, they were spending their days brushing the grass and painting the petals. Snufflewort were living happily with the animals of the garden, sharing tea and acorn cookies with the brownish squirrels and playing pullyball with the porcupine. Snufflewort even were doing the morning singing with the Robin bird, although the singing of Snufflewort is not being a sound that can be named as beautiful.

The days of Snufflewort had a changing when a Rumpa adventurer was becoming lost in the garden of many bending trees. Before this time, Snufflewort were always very forbidden to be speaking with Rumpa. It was told never to trust a creature with feet that are more bigger than the face of a Snufflewort. But when they were hearing the Rumpa adventurer calling through the wind of 10,000 leaves they could not stop but do helping. After Snufflewort were leading the Rumpa adventurer back to the path that was to her home, she was wanting to be thanking them with a feast of fire roasted pumpkins and honeyed lugg. This was the starting of the beginning of the promise of friendship between Snufflewort and Rumpa.

At the ending of the feast of pumpkin and lugg, Rumpa were inviting Snufflewort to become guardians of their green spaces. Snufflewort were being curious of the garden with straight lines for tulips and hedges shaped like wooden boxes, so they stayed with their new Rumpa friends, not returning to their wild growing places.

Snufflewort were being happy in their new friendship and the ways of the garden with many rules. They were having extra joyful when they could be tickling seeds in the dirt with the laughter of Rumpa children for a song. When the moon was a circle, Snufflewort would be chasing the weeds from the gardens and Rumpa would be serving tiny pickle sandwiches to thank their friends for their labouring.

But after the many years of happy passing, a darkness was coming. Rumpa were no longer working as the guardians of their own green spaces, they were always being busy with making their sometimes noisy inventions. Many of the contraptions were creating happy moments for Snufflewort, like a merry-go-round, that made your eyes dizzy but your heart float from spinning. But Rumpa were seeming to love some inventions more than the sun after a storm, like the television boxes and the machine that magically turned dirty dishes into sparkling ones. It came to be that Rumpa were more caring about the inside of their houses and having the chairs to be sitting on instead of the wooden stumps. They were stopping to talk with neighbours and they even were forgetting how to be speaking to Snufflewort.

Eventually Rumpa had lost the memory that they had been inviting Sunfflewort to be guardians of their green spaces. They invented the horrifying lawn muncher that was eating and spitting the grass. The Rumpa also had stopped the eating of fruits from their greenspaces. Instead of feasting on the pie of buckleberry they were tasting only the green vugga. A orb having the skin of a lizard, an inside like mud and a seed so big it could be choking a full grown Snufflewort. Never has a Snufflewort known the secret of growing the green vugga.

There were told some stories of great sadness when Rumpa would be throwing their Snufflewort into a horrible hole that has the name dumper. Many Snufflewort were being lost to the eyes of those that love them after disappearing into a dumper forever.

The ones that were surviving had to be hiding in the garden to stay safe from the claws of the new great friend of Rumpa, the cat.

At the time when the rainbow tulips made blooming no more, Snufflewort decided they must be calling on the crafts of the ones who had been before. In the book of "Things Snufflewort Can and Can Not Do", the secret of circle wafters had been written down. How water and magic were becoming portals to a different galaxy of green spaces. Snufflewort now are dreaming to be finding and freeing their brothers and sisters and travelling with them to a home where they can once again be painting the petals and brushing the grass in the morning.

CHAPTER 6

"I was right about the portal," said Yacob with satisfaction before taking another bite of his tuna bun. He always ate his sandwich first, so that he could progress from the worst to the best parts of his lunch in order. "The bubbles can carry some creatures to a different place in the universe." In his head Yacob hadn't quite figured out whether Snufflewort were like humans or something else completely, like a stuffie that could talk and sneeze and needed rescuing.

Hayda looked up from her sandwich, "And lizards?"

"What about lizards?" asked Yacob while chewing on the bland tasting bread and fish. He was already thinking about the pumpkin chocolate-chip muffin in his lunch that would soon make the trip to his stomach.

"Can the bubbles carry lizards to another place in the universe?" replied Hayda with irritation that Yacob wasn't following her thinking.

Yacob paused to consider Hayda's question, "I am really not sure about lizards, they wiggle a lot and have those pointy tails. Doesn't seem like they would be the best bubble travellers."

"Oh," responded Hayda with disappointment. She put the crusts of her own sandwich back into her plastic container. Yacob sensed his best friend's interest had been lost, like a lizard that had run away to find a sunnier spot in the pavement.

Longing to tell Hayda about Grumpy Schlumpy and the rescue plan and the fact that Snufflewort had been practising making bubbles or circle wafters in the pipes of his house, Yacob instead chewed on his carrot sticks. His sister had made him pinky promise not to tell anyone about their weekend adventures. And even though his sister was usually the most annoying person he had ever met, he now felt like their shared mission made her almost cool to be around. It was like they were knights who

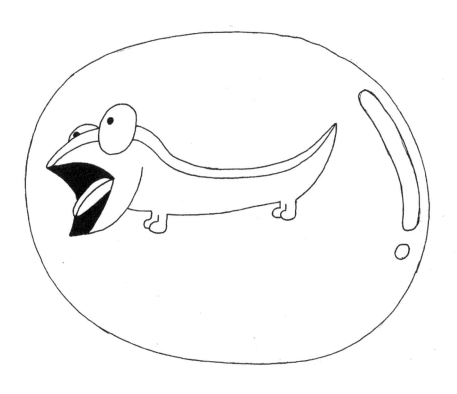

lived in castles and went on adventures with horses. Except instead of horses for companions, Yacob and Baley had Snufflewort.

Their rescue mission was set to take place on the coming Saturday after dinner, and the week at school was passing very slowly. Learning the difference between "their", "there" and "they're" was beyond boring during regular times, but this week Yacob watched Mr. Beverage prance in front of the whiteboard without really following the words that were coming out of his mouth. When Yacob did manage to pay attention to the grammar lessons, it only confirmed his belief that the person who created the rules for the English language should get an award for not following their own rules. Kind of like parents and television.

As it turned out, Yacob and Baley didn't have to wait until the end of the week to see the Snufflewort again. Wednesday after school Yacob went straight into the bathroom after arriving home. He needed to wash his face after giving himself a third eyebrow with a blue marker while day-dreaming, or day-nightmaring, during art class. He had been imagining what the inside of Grumpy Schlumpy's house looked like, picturing that it was full of spiderwebs big enough to catch nosy children. He wasn't sure if there were giant spiders too, or if Grumpy Schlumpy spun the webs himself.

However, when he turned on the bathroom taps, bubbles once again came pouring out. But rather than being shocked or even frightened this time, Yacob recognized the agreed emergency signal from the Snufflewort. After turning off the taps quickly so he wouldn't waste the magic, the almost eight-and-a-half year old ran to tell his sister they needed to meet Bob and Cosimo in the backyard right away.

Forgetting the rule about always knocking, Yacob flung open the door to his sister's bedroom and announced, "There's an emergency! We have to meet the Snufflewort! They sent the bubble signal!"

It was only after he had been standing by the open door for a few moments that he noticed the piles of purple papers stacked around his sister who was sitting on her bedroom floor.

"What are you doing?" Yacob asked with curiosity.

Baley grabbed her sweater from the floor and swept past Yacob while mumbling, "It's better you don't know."

Usually when his sibling refused to share a secret, Yacob felt a bit rejected. But this time, it actually seemed like she was trying to keep him safe from something dangerous. And that actually made him feel worse.

However, the sight of the two Snufflewort waiting in the backyard pushed thoughts of the stacks of purple paper out of Yacob's mind. The two Snufflewort were rocking back and forth in their leather boots with impatience.

Bob was the first to speak, "We are having a large danger alert!"

"We do, we do!" chimed in Cosimo, his braids flapping around while he shook his head with worry.

Yacob wondered if this was when perhaps the dragons came into the story. Or the truth that Grumpy Schlumpy was a spider who snacked on children.

Bob looked around suspiciously, making sure that their only audience was a soccer ball and a garden rake. He then continued, "In front of the house where our brothers and sisters have been trapped in a sack, we have been spotting something so full of terrible, so full of horrible!"

"It was a sign..." continued Bob while Cosimo looked on with terror, "... a sign for the horror of a yard sale!"

Yacob glanced at his sister to see if she looked as confused as he felt. As far as he could remember, yard sales usually just involved grown-ups picking through tables full of mismatched dishes and books with faded covers. He thought the only real danger from people selling old junk in their driveway was being forced to listen to another story from a parent about back-in-the-day after they discover a toy they used to own.

But now even Bob's arms were starting to flap in frustration at the lack of alarm from Baley and Yacob.

"When a Rumpa is having a yard sale, they are not actually doing a selling of the yard. They are doing a selling of the things that might be coming from the yard or basement. Like the tables with three legs .... like Snufflewort! Our tragic brothers and sisters might be bought and carried away in the dark trunks of cars by the strangers. And then we will never have eyes on them again," Bob whisper-shouted. "How will we be travelling together in a circle wafter to a new garden galaxy to brush the grass in the morning?"

"And there is a worse future also," added a trembling Cosimo.

"There is very worse," agreed Bob. "Are you knowing what is the fate of broken chairs and toasters that are not getting bought by strangers at a yard sale?"

Baley and Yacob didn't dare speak for fear they would further upset the Snufflewort. The siblings just shook their heads to indicate their ignorance.

"The chairs and toasters and Snufflewort are ending up in the dumper!" shrieked Bob.

A dumper seemed to be just about the worst thing that could happen to a Snufflewort. Even worse than a basement that the sun didn't know how to find. Yacob imagined that, for a Snufflewort, a dumper was a place with no exit. Like the way a vacuum sucked up toys and refused to give them back.

With the news that the yard sale was going to take place on Saturday morning, Baley made the decision that they would need to carry out their Snufflewort rescue mission on Friday.

But moving their mission from a weekend to a school day meant that the siblings were going to have to do something they had never done before. And if their mother ever found out she might just cancel Christmas and dessert forever. Yacob hoped the Snufflewort appreciated that he was risking a future without pumpkin chocolate chip muffins to save them.

CHAPTER 7

A tummy bug seemed like the hardest lie to prove was a lie. For a fever you had to be hot and sweaty. And a cold required sniffles and sneezing. But for a stomach flu Yacob and Baley only needed to claim to be on the cliff-edge of barfing. And according to Baley it wouldn't be surprising that they were both sick because vomiting was very contagious. Like children both coming down with an allergy to sleep the night before Christmas.

When Baley had explained the benefits of imaginary barfing to her brother she added that their mom would be extra worried about sending them to school. A fever in a classroom is hard to spot, a runny nose is easy to ignore, but if a child vomits all over their "Countries of the World" worksheet, that news is going to spread faster than head lice in a kindergarten classroom. And Baley was confident that the shame of being the parent who sent their barfing child to school would be enough to convince their mother to keep them home.

It turned out that Yacob and Baley's mother didn't need much persuading to let them skip school. She was distracted on Friday morning, saying she had an important meeting with a writer. According to their mother, this author didn't like feedback so she was quite nervous to tell them that their last chapter needed some "tweaking".

Yacob wasn't quite sure what "tweaking" meant, but it sounded like when a boy in Grade 4 pinched and twisted his skin while still managing to pick his own nose. It had hurt a lot and Yacob was pretty sure the writer wasn't going to like that even if his mother didn't pick her own nose.

Their mother was concerned enough about her fake-sick children to hover upstairs for most of the morning, but finally retreated to her basement office after serving them chicken broth and ginger ale for lunch. Still hungry after the watery soup and fizzy soda, Yacob was grateful that he had fourteen mini Choco Chew candy bars left over from Halloween. He didn't want his stomach to be yelling louder than his brain while he was trying to save the Snufflewort. He already had a guilty conscience making quite a bit of noise about the fact that he had lied about being sick to their mother for the first time ever.

About ten minutes after his mother had gone downstairs, there was a quick knock on Yacob's bedroom door. Without waiting for an answer, his sister walked in with a toque already on her head.

"Let's go," urged Baley. "Mom's meeting will probably last about an hour, so we don't have much time."

Already changed out of his pyjamas, Yacob threw off his blankets and tiptoed out of the room while avoiding stepping on the Choco Chew wrappers that now littered the floor. He reminded himself to pick up the evidence of his unhealthy feeding of his healthy appetite when he got back.

Yacob and Baley once more met the two Snufflewort in the backyard.

Both Bob and Cosimo were now wearing small green felt hats instead of pointy red ones. Maybe this was their idea of camouflage. Looking over, Yacob realized his sister was also wearing a green fleece and dark blue jeans. The almost-eight-and-a-half-year-old regretted putting on his yellow and black striped jacket. He was about as invisible as a 70 pound bumble bee.

"Have you been having success with your task of the mission?" asked Bob in a serious voice.

"'The plan for 'Exit Grumpy Schlumpy' has been executed," replied Baley in an equally serious tone.

His sister and the Snufflewort seemed like they knew all the rules for how to dress and how to talk during a secret mission. Yacob rubbed the metal of the Slip Slider in his pocket, hoping it would give him some confidence.

Baley then demanded, "What about your task, 'Invade The Home of Grumpy Schlumpy?'"

Yacob's breath caught in his throat. Although the group had already agreed to a plan, he thought when it came down to carrying out the actual rescue, his sister might still dream up some other way to rescue the Snufflewort. A way that didn't require him to actually go into the unhappy basement of Grumpy Schlumpy.

Cosimo answered Baley's question this time. "We have been inviting our secret weapon to make the invasion possible!"

And before Baley and Yacob could ask about the secret weapon, the two Snufflewort sneezed. When Baley and Yacob reopened their eyes, a third Snufflewort was standing next to Cosimo. This Snufflewort was much smaller, and could have been a child, except that it also had a beard.

"Baley and Yacob, this is the Snufflewort who carries the name Cleo," announced Bob.

"Nice to meet you. I'm Yacob," said Yacob, but then felt a bit silly. This wasn't a sharing circle from the first day of kindergarten.

But the smaller Snufflewort didn't seem bothered by Yacob's polite introduction, and simply made a deep bow in response.

"Just to clarify," asked Baley, "this is your secret weapon? An even smaller Snufflewort?"

Bob looked offended. "You Rumpa are always doing measuring by size. Big homes, big trucks, big chewing lawn mowers that are flossing their teeth with the stems of the daisies!"

Bob stopped for a moment, trying to calm himself.

"What does it mattering how big you are? What we are needing for this moment is small! Small and bouncy and brave."

Yacob had never read a story with a hero or a secret weapon that was described as small, bouncy and brave. But a week ago he also didn't hold meetings in the backyard with creatures that looked like a cross between his grandpa and a Christmas ornament.

Bob then asked, "Shall we begin the beginning?"

Baley nodded in return, "Let's begin."

The children and the Snufflewort once again made the journey across the neighbour's grass to reach the backyard of Grumpy Schlumpy. The house looked quiet and empty. But Yacob was still feeling very nervous about actually going inside.

"How do you know he isn't there?" Yacob turned to his sister.

Baley gave her brother a knowing look and said, "Because I left this flyer on his porch yesterday." She then pulled a folded piece of purple paper out of her pocket and passed it to her brother.

Curious, Jacob read over the words printed on the paper in large bold letters.

SILVER CREEK SUGAR COOKIES

2 for 1 sale

ONE HOUR ONLY

Friday Nov. 8th at

COUNTRY FOODS

1:00 - 2:00 pm

"How do you know Grumpy Schlumpy likes Silver Creek Sugar Cookies?" asked Yacob.

"It's the power of observation, little brother, the power of observation," Baley replied with a smile. "Do you remember seeing all those cookie tins in Grumpy Schlumpy's basement, next to the tied-up Snufflewort?"

"Yes. I mean, I guess so," responded Yacob.

"Well I recognized them from grandma's house. She loves the same brand. So I figured if we made Grumpy Schlumpy believe there was a one-hour sale of his favourite sugar cookies at the supermarket, he wouldn't be able to resist. You see, old folks, they love a sale. For them it's like Christmas, but you get boring things like toilet paper. But, unfortunately, the only thing old folks like better than a sale is a yard sale. That's why we have to get those

Snufflewort out of the basement before tomorrow morning."

Although he was impressed with his sister's resourcefulness, Yacob wasn't yet entirely convinced. "But the store is only a few blocks away. What if he just goes inside, sees there isn't a sale, and comes back home in 15 minutes?"

Baley flashed her brother a confident smile, "First he will have to get through the line-up of other old folks who also think there is a sale on sugar cookies. You see, I dropped about 50 flyers at the retirement home across the street from the grocery store. Grumpy Schlumpy could be standing in line for hours before he realizes the flyer is a fake."

Yacob recalled the sight of his sister sitting on her bedroom floor two days ago, surrounded by piles of purple papers. He wondered if delivering those flyers counted as telling one lie or 51.

"Is the time correct to be sending in our secret weapon?" asked Bob, who had been looking around anxiously while the siblings were talking.

"Send in the secret weapon," confirmed Baley.

On Baley's signal, the smallest of the Snufflewort approached Grumpy Schlumpy's backdoor. Yacob wondered if the small creature was going to pick the lock with some magic tools or perhaps use Snufflewort-sized dynamite to blow down the door. Instead, Cleo grabbed on to the bottom of the cat door and swung her tiny body through the plastic flap.

Impressed and slightly disappointed by the explosion-free entry of the Snufflewort, Yacob then heard a sound coming from the other side of the door that could only be described as bouncing. And after a few soft thuds followed by a clang, the backdoor to the house swung open. The small Snufflewort had jumped up to unlock the door and was hanging onto the handle like it was a roller coaster ride at the world's most boring amusement park.

Baley then looked at her brother and said, "Let's go rescue some Snufflewort."

Feeling more fear than excitement, Yacob wished a giant bubble would carry him through a portal back to Mr. Beverage and Grade 3 math class. Subtraction no longer seemed so scary. At least not when compared to Grumpy Schlumpy's open backdoor.

CHAPTER 8

Last Halloween, Yacob's mother had said he was old enough to buy a ticket for a tour of a haunted house along with his sister. Yacob's excitement to go inside the old, sagging house with torn curtains and top floor windows that looked like two evil eyes was immediately squelched by the fear that he had to go inside the old sagging house with torn curtains and evil-window eyes. To his total embarrassment, he spent the entire tour hiding his own eyes in the hood of his panda costume while also holding his sister's hand so he wouldn't bump into any dead mummies or evil broom sticks. In an attempt to drown out the screams and cackles, he loudly hummed the theme to the Slip Sliders TV show until he stumbled out the backdoor exit into a yard full of fake tombstones. Yacob was incredibly grateful and a little surprised that his sister had never once teased him about how he had squeezed her hand in terror the entire time. It made him realize that older siblings could sometimes be like mini-parents that didn't make you eat brown toast when you really wanted white.

As he crossed over the doorstep into Grumpy Schlumpy's house, Yacob was hoping he would manage to be brave like Cleo, if not bouncy. Holding his sister's hand in a dark haunted house where no one could see you was one thing. But he would feel very humiliated to look so scared in front of creatures that barely reached his belly button.

To his immense relief there were no giant spider webs waiting to trap small children spun across the back hallway of Grumpy Schlumpy's house. In fact, as he moved through the house, Yacob was surprised by how tidy and clean everything looked. In his own home the living room was littered with toys plotting to trip tired parents and the kitchen counter was entirely clean once a week, and then only for five minutes. But Yacob noticed that inside Grumpy Schlumpy's house everything from old framed photographs to metal door handles was shiny with polishing. It was true that the furniture looked a little old fashioned and faded, but there was no mess or dirt anywhere. Grumpy Schlumpy may have been a child-eating ogre, but he was a child-eating ogre who was very good at vacuuming.

Even though they knew Grumpy Schlumpy was at the supermarket, lost in a crowd of angry old people demanding a deal on sugar cookies, the children and Snufflewort quietly tiptoed towards a wooden door that they guessed led to the basement. When they arrived, Baley reached forward and pulled the handle towards them.

SCREEEEEEEECH.

The door let out a loud, spooky creak that sounded like it had escaped from a horror movie and taken up living in the hinges of Grumpy Schlumpy's basement door. Yacob gripped the Slip Slider in his pocket a little harder and tried to resist asking his sister if he could hold her hand.

A set of wooden stairs led down to the dark basement where the unhappy Snufflewort awaited rescuing. But just as Baley was about to put her foot on the first step, she instead fell back with a giant sneeze.

"That's weird," remarked Baley as she rubbed her nose.

Yacob wondered if the universe wasn't making his sister sick in revenge for the two of them pretending to have the stomach flu that morning. But besides the fact that his heart was pounding with fear, Yacob otherwise felt OK. Maybe the universe was only going after his sister because she was obviously the team captain of lying.

Shaking her head as if to push away the sneezes, Baley continued her descent into the basement. With three Snufflewort behind him, Yacob thought he didn't have any other choice but to follow his sister.

Yacob was stepping off the bottom plank of the stairs when one of the Snufflewort pushed past him.

"Frank! Yasmine! Marta! Stumper! Fenry!" Cosimo yelled out with relief and joy while doing his best to hug each of the captive Snufflewort through the burlap sack.

As the children watched on, Bob reached into his beard and pulled out a pair of scissors that looked like they were big enough to give an oak tree a haircut.

"Standby everybody!" ordered Bob as he moved forward with the giant snippers. But just as he had the oversized blades poised to cut the sack's drawstring, Baley let out another oversized sneeze.

"Haaaa-cheeeeew."

Bob leapt back in surprise and knocked over a tower of empty Silver Creek sugar cookie tins.

The clatter and clang of dozens of tumbling metal lids and bottoms echoed through the old house. Clearly the cookie tins didn't know that the first rule of secret rescue missions was being very quiet during secret rescue missios.

Baley looked around apologetically. "I'm so sorry. It won't happen again. Must be the dusty basement."

Yacob didn't know what was going on with his sister, but as he looked around at the now messy, but otherwise spotless, basement of Grumpy Schlumpy, he knew that dust wasn't to blame.

Bob just shook his head in irritation and then quickly snipped the knotted rope at the top of the sack. As soon as the sack fell around their feet, the Snufflewort leaped up and gave Bob and Cosimo proper hugs. They would have hugged Cleo too, but she was too busy bouncing with happiness.

"Ok, this is great," interrupted Baley with a sniffle, "but we have to get out of here before Grumpy Schlumpy returns."

The gaggle of Snufflewort all nodded in unison and started following Baley towards the stairs. But Baley had just put her foot on the second step when she froze, causing Yacob and the trailing Snufflewort to bang up against each other.

"Why has the moving stopped?" demanded Bob from the rear.

Baley didn't speak but simply pointed upwards. Following the direction of her finger, the rest of the group looked up and saw that a large white ball of fur and claws was crouched at the top of the stairs. The cat, which managed to be both fluffy and scary, was like a white dragon, cutting them off from their only escape out of a dungeon.

While Baley started rapidly sneezing from her cat allergy, the Snufflewort began squawking with alarm.

"It is the arch enemy of the Snufflewort!" yelled Bob.

"The creature that all Snufflewort are being taught to fear!" added one of the recently freed Snufflewort.

"They are poking their talons in our bodies like we are a pin cushion! And if we are running, they are catching us and pouncing on our hurting heads," came another voice from the group of Snufflewort.

Cosimo piped up, "Not to mention they are leaving pee and other unwanted presents in our gardens."

Watching as the Snufflewort flapped their arms with panic, and his sister continued to sneeze uncontrollably, Yacob knew he had to take action. Gripping the Slip Slider in his pocket, he decided it was time to make a sacrifice.

Yacob pulled out his favourite black and red Slip Slider and held it up in the dim light of the basement. This Slip Slider had won Yacob more battles than he could count, but it was time to face a challenge outside of the arena. He had always known that one day he would use the Slip Slider to fight real danger. He just never imagined that danger would be wearing a leather collar with the name 'Snowball' printed on it.

Bending his wrist in a practised motion, Yacob flicked the Sip Slider out of his hand. With a flash, the metallic toy managed to reflect a few glimmers of light in the dark basement as it landed on the stairway's wooden railing and slid upwards. To the amazement of the onlooking group, when the Slip Slider reached the top of the railing it flew over the head of the shocked feline. And since the cat was a cat, it couldn't resist chasing after the toy which was more exciting than the invention of mice.

Baley managed to take a short break from sneezing to turn to Yacob and say, "Well done little brother. Well done."

Overcome once again with sneezing, Baley simply motioned for the group to follow her up the stairs and out the back door into the yard. As the newly freed Snufflewort hugged the grass, the sun seemed to cheer the group's successful mission by shining extra brightly that day.

CHAPTER 9

A baby blue autumn sky was visible through the partially opened bedroom curtains when Yacob woke up on Saturday morning. Snuggling under his covers, he thought through the list of possible ways he could spend his day. He might build a castle out of mini-bricks or hunt for worms in the front yard. He considered asking his sister to join him in a Slip Slider tournament, but he was still a little sad after losing his best battler yesterday in Grumpy Schlumpy's house. After thinking over the options, Yacob decided against pursuing a regular activity for an almost eight-and-a-half year old. Instead, he thought he would do something that old people like parents might do. He decided to go to a yard sale.

Yacob was hoping his sister would want to check out the sale in the driveway of Grumpy Schlumpy, but he worried she would still be sleeping-off the antihistamines she had taken after yesterday's encounter with the cat. Thankfully, when they had arrived home their mother had not yet finished her work. However, after a flurry of especially loud sneezes from Baley, their mother came quickly running up the stairs.

"I thought you had a stomach flu, but now it looks like allergies," their mother had stated while measuring out medicine for Baley. "When did you touch a cat?"

Yacob had assumed his sister was too overwhelmed with only having two hands with which to itch her whole body to come up with a good lie, so he had stepped into action.

"There was a cat in the school yard yesterday. It must have rubbed her scarf when she threw it on the ground while playing soccer." Yacob had wondered if being a convincing liar was something that ran in families - like being good at playing piano.

His mother had shook her head and said, "A cat? In the school yard? On her scarf? But why did she have her scarf in bed this morning?"

Thankfully a riot of sneezes from Baley had distracted their mother from asking any further questions. Instead she urged her daughter to get into the shower to wash off her skin and hair.

The following morning Yacob was still uncertain as to whether he should bother Baley so early. But after yesterday's adventures he felt braver than usual, so he marched up to his sister's bedroom door and knocked.

"Come in," his sister called from inside.

Opening the door, Yacob stepped inside and said, "Hey."

"Hey you," replied Baley. Her eyes were still a little red, but otherwise she looked mostly recovered.

"I was just wondering," continued Yacob despite feeling a little nervous, "I was wondering if you wanted to check out the yard sale."

Without taking a moment to consider, Baley responded with enthusiasm, "Absolutely! We need to do some post-secret mission surveillance. Find out if we left any incriminating evidence behind."

Yacob pictured his favourite Slip Slider in the jaws of the fluffy, yet dragon-like, cat.

As if guessing what her brother was thinking, Baley said, "Don't worry Yacob, I'll get you another Slip Slider. One of the new ones that has four rings instead of three. It'll be awesome."

By the time the two siblings had eaten breakfast and made it out of the house, there was already a crowd gathered in front of Grumpy Schlumpy's house. Yacob noticed that there weren't any children at the yard sale. Just old people like his mother - and even older.

The tables were covered with records, books and tea cups without saucers. There were even some wooden trains and tracks that children were probably forced to play with before Slip Sliders were invented. But by far the most interesting sight at the garage sale was Grumpy Schlumpy.

As the children gazed at their elderly neighbour, wearing a faded yellow cardigan, they both realized he had also been hiding a secret. Grumpy Schlumpy knew how to smile.

"Would you like a cookie?"

Still staring at the happy face of their neighbour in shock, Baley and Yacob were startled when they realized an old woman with white hair, lots of wrinkles and a kind voice had walked up to them. She was holding out a tin of Silver Creek Sugar Cookies with the lid off.

The siblings simply nodded and took a cookie each from the box. While they munched on the sweet buttery tasting treat the old woman continued talking.

"Aren't they delicious? They are my favourite kind." She took one out of the box as if to examine it up close.

"It is, however, so strange what happened at the supermarket yesterday. Everyone at the retirement home received flyers saying there was a cookie sale, but the store manager didn't know a thing about it." The woman took a bite of the cookie before getting on with her story.

"Finally, they decided to give us the cookies on sale anyway. I mean, you wouldn't want to cheese-off a big crowd of old people. Your Senior's Saturday discount would be as empty as a bingo hall that charges for tea.

Yacob let out a small giggle, he wondered if "cheesed-off" people came in different versions, like cheddar and mozzarella.

"Anyway," the old woman smiled broadly, "I better get back to helping Gustav. He is such a nice man, if perhaps a little lonely."

The old woman started to walk away from the children but then turned back and said, "And you know what? If it hadn't been for those odd flyers about the cookies being on sale even when they weren't, I never would have met Gustav. Well, thank goodness for that."

Just at that moment, Gustav, who the children knew as Grumpy Schlumpy, looked up and waved at the nice woman. She waved back and headed in his direction.

Yacob was now trying to figure out whether his sister was actually a good person for telling 51 lies to old people. Maybe sometimes the rules for right and wrong were a little mixed-up for kids too, just like parents breaking their own rules about TV. He wondered if his new friends ever stretched the rules in the book of *Things Snufflewort Can and Can Not Do*.

Once again Yacob's thoughts were interrupted by the voices of grown-ups.

"I am so sorry madam. I did have garden gnomes to sell, but somehow they have disappeared," apologized Grumpy Schlumpy to a couple wearing green vests and muddy boots, making them look like they were happiest in a garden. "Yesterday morning they were in my basement, but this morning, 'poof' they are gone. Either my old brain is playing tricks or it's some kind of magic."

Yacob and Baley looked on in amazement as Grumpy Schlumpy merrily described the extra peculiar and very unexplainable events in his own life.

"Oh, how strange and disappointing," said a tall woman to her shorter husband, "It would have been simply wonderful to have those creatures in our garden."

Turning back to Grumpy Schlumpy she added, "We live at Winder Place, at the bottom of Winder Lane."

Yacob and Baley weren't sure why the woman bothered to offer directions to her home. Everyone in their neighborhood knew Winder Place. It was a tall brick mansion built back-in-the-day when rich people had armies of servants to cook their meals, clean their homes and even play games with their children. Yacob sometimes wished his mother had an army to help her, or at least one good soldier who liked loading dishwashers instead of guns.

Winder Place was also famous because it had gardens that seemed to go on forever. The front yard had rows of flowers that were always in bloom. In the backyard, the leaves of Willow trees provided excellent hiding spots for playing hide and seek while the Oak trees had branches perfectly spaced for climbing. And no one seemed to mind that children played there.

Before the disappointed woman who lived at Winder Place walked away from the yard sale with her husband, she made a last request to Grumpy Schlumpy. "If you do manage to track down a few of those garden gnomes, please let us know."

With the mention of the escaped Snufflewort, Yacob and Baley decided to head back to their own backyard. They didn't say anything out loud, but the siblings were both a little afraid that their new friends had already left in a circle wafter to live in a greener, lawnmower-free spot in the galaxy.

Much to their relief, when they walked around the corner of their house into the backyard, Bob and Cosimo were standing in the middle of the grass, as if waiting for them to arrive.

Before Yacob and Baley could say anything, Cosimo ran forward and took turns hugging each of them around the knees. Feeling his chest tighten a little, Yacob had no idea his knees could have such strong emotions.

Bob was the first to speak.

"Wise and wonderful Rumpa, we are having no treasures enough to show thanks for your brave actions. We are wanting you to know that the names Baley and Yacob will be always honoured in the stories that are written by Snufflewort."

Feeling both very happy and very sad at the exact same moment, Yacob replied, "You're welcome." And then he added, "Adventuring is fun."

Since his sister was always keen to get down to business, Yacob wasn't surprised when Baley asked, "So when are you leaving, in your bubble thingies, to go through the portal?"

"We are making our departure this evening in our circle wafters. At dusk, when the power of the moon and the sun are being strongest together," replied Bob.

Yacob realized his sister really was right about everything cool happening at dusk.

"What is this new place called?" asked Baley, "In case we ever manage circle wafter travel for Rumpa."

Bob and Cosimo both burst into laughter.

"Circle wafter travelling for Rumpa?" giggled Cosimo while clutching his tiny sides with his tiny hands. "That's like imagining a cat you could love. It will never be in the possible."

Yacob wasn't so sure that Cosimo was right about cats being the enemies of the Snufflewort forever. If nasty Grumpy Schlumpy can turn into smiling Gustav, maybe it could happen.

Bob finally calmed down enough to answer Baley's questions.

"The name of the distant place in the galaxy which will become the new homeland of all Snufflewort is ... Mexico!"

"MEXICO!!!" yelled out Baley and Yacob in surprise.

"MEXICO?" The siblings repeated, this time in disbelief.

Bob looked very shocked. "You have heard of this most distant and beautiful space on the edge of another galaxy?"

"Yes," stated Baley. "We have been there twice for vacation."

"Really?" Bob looked confused and a little worried. "But isn't it on the other side of the universe?"

"No, it's just on the other side of the United States," said Baley. "And you should know, the gardens look a bit different in Mexico. It's pretty hot and dry, although I guess they manage to grow a lot of avocados."

"Avocados?" asked Cosimo with curiosity. "What are the avocados?"

Yacob was surprised such travellers of the universe had never met an avocado.

"You know, they are green, with lumpy skins and a big seed inside. My mom spreads them on toast," he said in a helpful voice.

"THE GREEN VUGGA!" Cosimo yelled in wild distress while flapping his arms.

"Not the dreaded green vugga," muttered Bob in a much quieter, but equally concerned voice. "What can we be doing? Where can we be going?! We are not growers of green vugga that made the Rumpa be stopping to love the fruit of their own gardens."

Yacob and Baley were both a bit taken aback. Although they both preferred chocolate spread on their toast rather than avocado, they had no idea that such a villain had been lurking in their fruit bowl.

While continuing to talk Bob stroked his beard as if trying to soothe himself. "The great dream of our new garden home is being broken and smashed on the ground like branches of a tree after an angry storm. Where will our children be learning to paint the daisies yellow? Where will my fellow Snufflewort be brushing the grass in the morning?"

Yacob looked over at his sister and was astonished to see a smile was returning to her face.

"Don't worry Bob and Cosimo," said Baley. "I have a plan."

CHAPTER 10

The children left their house again that Saturday at dusk, a time considered magical by many creatures both big and very small. It was also a time of day when it was harder for grown-ups to spot children mischievously pulling an overloaded wagon down the streets of their neighbourhood. The wagon was quite heavy so Baley did most of the pulling while Yacob kept a look-out for any inconveniently curious adults.

By the time they reached their destination, one of the wheels of the wagon was threatening to come loose. Yacob had to help his sister lift the wagon gently down the last curb, but still managed to bump it on the ground. From underneath the blanket that was covering the load, there was an eruption of giggles followed by a loud "shush."

Looking around one last time to make sure the coast was clear, Baley then lifted the blanket off the wagon to reveal a gaggle of Snufflewort in a topsy turvy pile. Cosimo's braid was lying under Bob's nose like a mustache, and the Snufflewort named Fenry had his feet on the head of Stumper.

Baley and Yacob lifted the Snufflewort one by one out of the wagon except for Cleo who easily bounced onto the ground without assistance. Once everyone was standing on their own two small feet, the group walked under large looming gates that opened into a sprawling lush garden.

"It's called Winder Place," said Baley. "Yacob and I sometimes play here on sunny days."

Bob marched out ahead of the group, surveying the trees, lawn and bushes with a serious gaze.

"It is the autumn season now, but the flower beds are being well dressed for their winter sleep," he commented, while continuing to investigate further into the garden.

"These trees are having strong branches and the soil is being healthy, but the one who is pruning the branches has not been attending their task."

While Bob was talking, the other Snufflewort were spreading out through the garden to conduct their own inspections. But from the occasional giggle and squeal, they seemed to be a little less serious than Bob in their survey. With blades of grass now braided into his hair, Cosimo came skipping up to where Bob, Yacob and Baley were standing.

"There are being three trees of lilac in the green space behind! I was sniffing the branches and it was revealed their colours are of white, lilac and burple," cried Cosimo with excitement.

Baley corrected, "You mean purple?"

Cosimo shook his head and said, "No I mean burple. But you are a poor Rumpa, and are not knowing the difference between the smell of burple and purple."

Bob interrupted with a question for Baley. "How do you know we are being wanted to make a home here? How do you know we won't be ending our time in a sack in another dark bottom of a house? I think maybe we should be making a journey to a home in Mexico."

"Unless you want to be petting lizards in the morning instead of brushing grass, I would forget Mexico," replied Baley. "And we know you are wanted here. The people who own the house have been searching for garden gnomes, I mean Snufflewort."

Baley stopped talking in order to watch as a group of Snufflewort came running up to Bob as quickly as their short legs could carry them through the long grass.

"I found the roots of daisies under the apple tree," said Fenry excitedly.

"And there are seeds of lilies along the westerly path," added Yasmine.

Bob sighed and looked at the children and Snufflewort for a moment without talking. Then he took his red pointed hat off, itched his thick white hair, and put the hat back on. Only then did he start to speak, while stroking his beard.

"Snufflewort, small Rumpa. I have been making a decision in my mind. We will be creating our new home in the place that has the name Windy Place," stated Bob in his best, most serious voice.

"It's actually Winder Place," corrected Baley, but an annoyed look from Bob made it clear the correction was not appreciated.

Bob then continued with his speech, "Windy Place will be becoming the home of the Snufflewort. We will be calling our brother and sister Snufflewort who are in other lost places to be joining us in the garden of many flowers and well-growing trees."

The gaggle of Snufflewort did what can only be described as a Snufflewort dance in reaction to the news of their new home. Then Baley and Yacob watched as the Snufflewort once again spread out across the garden to sniff the soil and inspect the roots of trees.

The sky was darkening and the siblings knew it was time to go home. Yacob realized that secret missions that required occasional lying for a good reason were really quite exhausting. He was look-ing forward to a bedtime story with his mom, maybe one without any dragons. He only wished he could share their Snufflewort ad-ventures with her since she would probably enjoy a break from thinking about demanding dishwashers and even more demand-ing authors. Thinking of all his mother's adult responsibilities, Yacob promised himself he would stay almost eight-and-a-half years old for as long as possible.

"Good luck," Yacob said in farewell to the Snufflewort. He wasn't really sure what kind of good-bye was right for this situation, since he had never before said good-bye after rescuing small crea-tures in pointy hats from a neighbour's dungeon that was guarded by a white fluffy dragon-cat and then found them a new garden home full of grass to be brushed in the morning.

"Thank you and good-bye small Rumpa," replied Bob.

"If you ever need us again," said Baley, "You can always do the bub-ble thing. I mean the circle wafters."

Bob nodded but then added, "I think we will be finding happiness in the blossoms and branches of this garden. But many thanks for the bravery in your heart."

Once the good-byes had been spoken, Yacob and Baley turned to go, pulling the wagon behind them. The limping wheel made it seem as though the wagon was also a little sad to see the adven-ture end.

But then suddenly, when the siblings were just about to turn right, in the direction of their home, Cosimo came running after them, his braids swinging with excitement.

"Wait, Rumpa, please wait."

The two children stopped and waited for the Snufflewort to catch up. Holding up his clenched right hand, Cosimo spread open his fingers to reveal what he was holding.

Resting in the centre of the creature's small palm was Yacob's lost Slip Slider. A streak of red from the late November sunset made the toy shimmer almost magically in the fading light of dusk.

"My Slip Slider!" exclaimed Yacob with delight and relief.

"The cat was burying it in the garden," explained Cosimo. "But don't worry, I was washing off all the catness from it."

Holding his cherished toy tightly in his hand, Yacob whispered, "Thank you." Two words that were too small to express all the joy pumping through his brave but tired Rumpa heart.

He wondered if the knights who rode horses and rescued innocent creatures from dungeons knew that the best treasure is the one you thought you had lost.

THE END

Made in the USA
Monee, IL
24 September 2021

78212461R10046